THE

WERE-

WOLF

THE WERE-WOLF

AND OTHER TALES FROM THE
DARK SIDE OF THE MOON

EDITED BY JOHN MILLER AND TIM SMITH

CHRONICLE BOOKS
SAN FRANCISCO

Printed in Singapore.

Library of Congress Cataloging-in-Publication Data:
The Were-wolf / edited by John Miller & Tim Smith.
           p.   cm.
         ISBN 0-8118-1131-X
    1. Werewolves—Literary collections.
   I. Miller, John, 1959-   . II. Smith, Tim, 1962-   .
         PN6071.W47W47   1995
         808.8'0375—dc20   95-12954
                                    CIP

Editing and design: Big Fish Books
Composition: Jennifer Petersen, Big Fish Books

Distributed in Canada by Raincoast Books,
8680 Cambie Street, Vancouver, B.C. V6P 6M9

10 9 8 7 6 5 4 3 2 1

Chronicle Books
275 Fifth Street
San Francisco, CA 94103

THANKS TO

KIRSTEN MILLER

SHELLEY BERNIKER

CONTENTS

PREFACE

O H! YE IMMORTAL Gods!
What is Theogony?
Oh! thou, too, mortal man!
what is philosophy?
Oh! World, which was and is, what is
Cosmogony?
Some people have accused me of
Misanthropy;
And yet I know no more than the mahogany
That forms this desk, of what they

mean;—Lycanthropy

I comprehend, for without transformation

Men become wolves on any slight occasion.

THE
WOLF

HERE IS WHAT the old Marquis d'Arville told us towards the end of St. Hubert's dinner at the house of the Baron des Ravels.

We had killed a stag that day. The marquis was the only one of the guests who had not taken any part in this chase, for he never hunted.

All through that long repast we had talked about hardly anything but the slaughter of animals. The ladies themselves were interested in tales sanguinary and often unlikely, and the orators imitated the attacks and the combats of men against beasts, raised their arms, romanced in a thundering voice.

M. d'Arville talked well, with a certain poetry of style somewhat high-sounding, but full of effect. He must have repeated this story often, for he told it fluently, not hesitating on words, choosing them with skill to produce a picture—

Gentlemen, I have never hunted; neither did my father, nor my grandfather, nor my great-grandfather. This last was the son of a man who hunted more than all of you put together. He died in 1764. I will tell you how.

His name was Jean. He was married,

father of that child who became my ancestor, and he lived with his younger brother, François d'Arville, in our castle in Lorraine, in the middle of the forest.

François d'Arville had remained a bachelor for love of the chase.

They both hunted from one end of the year to the other, without repose, without stopping, without fatigue. They loved only that, understood nothing else, talked only of that, lived only for that.

They had at heart that one passion, which was terrible and inexorable. It consumed them, having entirely invaded them, leaving place for no other.

They had given orders that they should not be interrupted in the chase, for any reason whatever. My great-grandfather was born while his father was following a fox, and Jean d'Arville did not stop his pursuit, but he swore: "Name of a name, that rascal there might have waited till after the view-halloo!"

His brother Francois showed himself still more infatuated. On rising he went to see the dogs, then the horses; then he shot little birds about the castle until the moment for departing to hunt down some great beast.

In the countryside they were called M. le Marquis and M. le Cadet, the nobles then not doing at all like the chance nobility of our time, which wishes to establish an hereditary hierarchy in titles; for the son of a marquis is no more of a count, nor the son of a viscount a

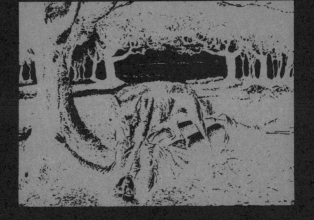

baron, than the son of a general is a colonel by birth. But the mean vanity of today finds profit in that arrangement.

I return to my ancestors.

They were, it seems, immeasurably tall, bony, hairy, violent, and vigorous. The younger, still taller than the older, had a voice so strong that, according to a legend of which he was proud, all the leaves of the forests shook when he shouted.

And when they both mounted to go off to hunt, that must have been a superb spectacle to see those two giants straddling their huge horses.

Now towards the midwinter of that year, 1764, the frosts were excessive, and the wolves became ferocious.

They even attacked belated peasants, roamed at night about the houses, howled from sunset to sunrise, and depopulated the stables.

And soon a rumor began to circulate. People talked of a colossal wolf, with gray fur, almost white, who had eaten two children, gnawed off a woman's arm, strangled all the dogs of the *guarde du pays*, and penetrated without fear into the farm-yards to come snuffling under the doors. The people in the houses affirmed that they had felt his breath, and that it made the flame of the lights flicker. And soon a panic ran through all the province. No one dared go out any more after night-fall. The shades seemed haunted by the image of the beast.

The brothers d'Arville resolved to find and kill him, and several times they assembled all the gentlemen of the country to a great hunting.

In vain. They might beat the forest and search the coverts; they never met him. They killed wolves, but not that one. And every night after a *battue*, the beast, as if to avenge himself, attacked some traveller or devoured someone's cattle, always far from the place where they had looked for him.

Finally one night he penetrated into the pig-pen of the Château d'Arville and ate the two finest pigs.

The brothers were inflamed with anger, considering this attack as a bravado of the monster, an insult direct, a defiance. They took their strong blood-hounds used to pursue formidable beasts, and they set off to hunt, their hearts swollen with fury.

From dawn until the hour when the empurpled sun descended behind the great naked trees, they beat the thickets without finding anything.

At last, furious and disconsolate, both were returning, walking their horses along an *allée* bordered with brambles, and they marvelled that their woodcraft should be crossed so by this wolf, and they were seized suddenly with a sort of mysterious fear.

The elder said:

"That beast there is not an ordinary one. You would say it thought like a man."

The younger answered:

"Perhaps we should have a bullet blessed by our cousin, the bishop, or pray some priest to pronounce the words which are needed."

Then they were silent.

Jean continued:

"Look how red the sun is. The great wolf will do some harm tonight."

He had hardly finished speaking

when his horse reared; that of François began to kick. A large thicket covered with dead leaves opened before them, and a colossal beast, quite gray, sprang up and ran off across the wood.

Both uttered a kind of groan of joy, and, bending over the necks of their heavy horses, they threw them forward with an impulse from their whole bodies, hurling them on at such a pace, exciting them, hurrying them away, maddening them so with the voice, with gesture, and with spur that the strong riders seemed rather to be carrying the heavy beasts between their thighs and to bear them off as if they were flying.

Thus they went, *ventre à terre*, bursting the thickets, cleaving the beds of stream, climbing the hillsides, descending the gorges, and blowing on the horn with full lungs to attract their people and their dogs.

And now, suddenly, in that mad race, my ancestor struck his forehead against an enormous branch which split his skull; and he fell stark dead on the ground, while his frightened horse took himself off, disappearing in the shade which enveloped the woods.

The cadet of Arville stopped short, leaped to the earth, and seized his brother in his arms. He saw that the brains ran from the wound with the blood.

Then he sat down beside the body, rested the head, disfigured and red, on his knees, and waited, contemplating that immobile face of the elder brother. Little by little a fear invaded him, a strange fear which he had never felt before, the fear of the dark, the fear of solitude, the fear of the deserted wood, and the fear also of the fantastic wolf who had just killed his brother to avenge himself upon them both.

The shadows thickened; the acute cold made the trees crack. Francois got up,

shivering, unable to remain there longer, feeling himself almost growing faint. Nothing was to be heard, neither the voice of the dogs nor the sound of the horns—all was silent along the invisible horizon; and this mournful silence of the frozen night had something about it frightening and strange.

He seized in his colossal hands the great body of Jean, straightened it and laid it across the saddle to carry it back to the château; then he went on his way softly, his mind troubled as if he were drunken, pursued by horrible and surprising images.

And abruptly, in the path which the night was invading, a great shape passed. It was the beast. A shock of terror shook the hunter; something cold, like a drop of water, glided along his veins, and, like a monk haunted of the devil, he made a great sign of the cross, dismayed at this abrupt return of the frightful prowler. But his eyes fell back upon the inert body laid before him, and suddenly, passing abruptly from fear to anger, he shook with an inordinate rage.

Then he spurred his horse and rushed after the wolf.

He followed it by the copses, the ravines, and the tall trees, traversing woods which he no longer knew, his eyes fixed on the white speck which fled before him through the night now fallen upon the earth.

His horse also seemed animated by a force and an ardor hitherto unknown. It galloped, with outstretched neck, straight on, hurling against the trees, against the rocks, the head and the feet of the dead man thrown across the saddle. The briers tore out the hair; the brow, beating the huge trunks, spattered them with blood; the spurs tore their ragged coats of bark. And suddenly the beast and the horseman issued from the forest and rushed into a valley, just as the moon appeared above the mountains. This valley was stony, closed by enormous rocks, without possible issue; and the wolf was cornered and turned round.

François then uttered a yell of joy which the echoes repeated like a rolling of thunder, and he leaped from his horse, his cutlass in his hand.

The beast, with bristling hair, the back arched, awaited him; its eyes glistened like two stars. But, before offering battle, the strong hunter, seizing his brother, seated him on a rock, and, supporting with stones his head, which was no more than a blot of blood, he shouted in the ears as if he was talking to a deaf man, "Look, Jean; look at this!"

Then he threw himself upon the monster. He felt himself strong enough to overturn a mountain, to bruise the stones in his hands. The beast tried to bite him, seeking to strike in at his stomach; but he had seized it by the neck, without even using his weapon, and he strangled it gently, listening to the stoppage of the breathings in its throat and the beatings of its heart. And he laughed, rejoicing madly, pressing closer and closer his formidable embrace, crying in a delirium of joy, "Look, Jean, look!" All resistance ceased; the body of the wolf became lax. He was dead.

Then François, taking him up in his arms, carried him off and went and threw him at the feet of the elder brother, repeating, in a tender voice, "There, there, there, my little Jean, see him!"

Then he replaced on the saddle the two bodies one upon the other, and he went his way.

He returned to the château, laughing and crying, like Gargantua at the birth of Pantagruel, uttering shouts of triumph and stamping with joy in relating the death of the beast, and moaning and tearing his beard in telling that of his brother.

And often, later, when he talked again

of that day, he said, with tears in his eyes, "If only that poor Jean could have seen me strangle the other, he would have died content. I am sure of it!"

The widow of my ancestor inspired her orphan son with that horror of the chase which has transmitted itself from father to son as far down as myself.

The Marquis d'Arville was silent. Someone asked:

"That story is a legend, isn't it?"

And the storyteller answered:

"I swear to you that it is true from one end to the other."

Then a lady declared, in a little, soft voice:

"All the same, it is fine to have passions like that."

THE
WEREWOLF

IT IS A northern country; they have cold weather, they have cold hearts.

Cold; tempest; wild beasts in the forest. It is a hard life. Their houses are built of logs, dark and smoky within. There will be a crude icon of the virgin behind a guttering candle, the leg of a pig hung up to cure, a string of drying mushrooms. A bed, a stool, a table. Harsh, brief, poor lives.

To these upland woodsmen, the Devil

as far as you or I. More so, they have not seen us nor even know that we exist, but the Devil they glimpse often in the graveyards, those bleak and touching townships of the dead where the graves are marked with portraits of the deceased in the naïf style and there are no flowers to put in front of them, no flowers grow there, so they put out small, votive offerings, little loaves, sometimes a cake that the bears come lumbering from the margins of the forest to snatch away. At midnight, especially on Walpurgisnacht, the Devil holds picnics in the graveyards and invites the witches; then they dig up fresh corpses, and eat them. Anyone will tell you that.

Wreaths of garlic on the doors keep out the vampires. A blue-eyed child born feet first on the night of St. John's Eve will have second sight. When they discover a witch—some old woman whose cheeses ripen when her neighbours' do not, another old woman whose black cat, oh, sinister! *follows her about all the time*, they strip the crone, search for her marks, for the supernumerary nipple her familiar sucks. They soon find it. Then they stone her to death.

Winter and cold weather.

Go and visit grandmother, who has been sick. Take her the oatcakes I've baked for her on the hearthstone and a little pot of butter.

The good child does as her mother bids—five miles' trudge through the forest; do not leave the path because of the bears, the wild boar, the starving wolves. Here, take your father's hunting knife; you know how to use it.

The child had a scabby coat of sheep-skin to keep out the cold, she knew the forest too well to fear it but she must always be on her guard. When she heard that freezing howl of a wolf, she dropped her gifts, seized her knife and turned on the beast.

It was a huge one, with red eyes and running, grizzled chops; any but a moun-taineer's child would have died of fright at

the sight of it. It went for her throat, as
wolves do, but she made a great swipe at it
with her father's knife and slashed off its right
forepaw.

The wolf let out a gulp, almost a sob,
when it saw what had happened to it; wolves
are less brave than they seem. It went lollop-
ing off disconsolately between the trees as
well as it could on three legs, leaving a trail of
blood behind it. The child wiped the blade of
her knife clean on her apron, wrapped up the
wolf's paw in the cloth in which her mother
had packed the oatcakes and went on towards
her grandmother's house. Soon it came on to
snow so thickly that the path and any foot-
steps, track or spoor that might have been
upon it were obscured.

She found her grandmother was so sick she had taken to her bed and fallen into a fretful sleep, moaning and shaking so that the child guessed she had a fever. She felt the forehead, it burned. She shook out the cloth from her basket, to use it to make the old woman a cold compress, and the wolf's paw fell to the floor.

But it was no longer a wolf's paw. It was a hand, chopped off at the wrist, a hand toughened with work and freckled with old age. There was a wedding ring on the third finger and a wart on the index finger. By the wart, she knew it for her grandmother's hand.

She pulled back the sheet but the old woman woke up, at that, and began to struggle, squawking and shrieking like a thing possessed. But the child was strong, and armed with her father's hunting knife; she managed to hold her grandmother down long enough to see the cause of her fever. There was a bloody stump where her right hand should have been, festering already.

The child crossed herself and cried out so loud the neighbours heard her and come rushing in. They knew the wart on the hand at once for a witch's nipple; they drove the old woman, in her shift as she was, out into the snow with sticks, beating her old carcass as far as the edge of the forest, and pelted her with stones until she fell dead.

Now the child lived in her grandmother's house; she prospered.

LYCAON AND JUPITER

LYCAON, KING OF *Arcadia, in
order to discover if it is Jupiter himself
who has come to lodge in his palace,
orders the body of an hostage, who had been sent to
him, to be dressed and served up at a feast. The God,
as a punishment, changes him into a wolf.*

I had *now* passed Maenalus, to be dreaded for
its dens of beasts of prey, and the pine-groves
of cold Lycaeus, together with Cyllene. After

this, I entered the realms and the inhospitable abode of the Arcadian tyrant, just as the late twilight was bringing on the night. I gave a signal that a God had come, and the people commenced to pay their adorations. In the first place, Lycaon derided their pious suppli-cations. Afterwards, he said, I will make trial, by a plain proof, whether this is a God, or whether he is a mortal; nor shall the truth remain a matter of doubt. He then makes preparations to destroy me, when sunk in sleep, by an unexpected death; this mode of testing the truth pleases him. And not con-tent with that, with the sword he cuts the throat of an hostage that had been sent from the nation of the Molossians, and then softens part of the quivering limbs in boiling water, and part he roasts with fire placed beneath. Soon as he had placed these on the table, I, with avenging flames, overthrew the house upon the household Gods, worthy of their master. Alarmed, he himself takes to flight, and having reached the solitude of the country, he howls aloud, and in vain attempts to speak; his mouth gathers rage from himself, and through its *usual* desire for slaughter, it is directed against the sheep, and even still delights in blood. His garments are changed into hair, his arms into legs; he becomes a wolf, and he still retains vestiges of his ancient form. His hoariness is still the same, the same violence *appears* in his features; his eyes are bright as before; *he is still* the same image of ferocity.

"Thus fell one house; but one house alone did not deserve to perish; wherever the earth extends, the savage Erinnys reigns. You would suppose that men had conspired to be wicked; let all men speedily feel that vengeance which they deserve to endure, for such is my determination."

— *Translated by Henry T. Riley*

STUBBE
PEETER

O R, A T R U E Discourse
Declaring the Life and Death of One
Stubbe Peeter,

A Most Wicked Sorcerer, Who in the Likeness of a Wolf

Committed Many Murders,

Continuing This Devilish Practise 25 Years,

Killing and Devouring Men, Women, and Children.

Who for the Same Fact Was Taken and Executed

the 31st of October Last Past

in the *Town of Bedbur Near the City of Collin in Germany.*

Truly translated out of the high Dutch, according to the copy printed in Collin, brought over into England by George Bores ordinary post, the 11th day of this present month of June 1590, who did both see and hear the same.

I N THE TOWNS of Cperadt and Bedbur near Collin in high Germany, there was continually brought up and nourished one Stubbe Peeter, who from his youth was greatly inclined to evil and the practising of wicked arts, surfeiting in the damnable desire of magic, necromancy, and sorcery, acquainting himself with many infernal spirits and fiends. The Devil, who hath a ready ear to listen to the lewd motions of cursed men, promised to give him whatsoever his heart desired during his mortal life: whereupon this vile wretch, having a tyrannous heart and a most cruel bloody mind, requested that at his pleasure he might work his malice on men, women, and children, in the shape of some beast, whereby he might live without dread or danger of life, and unknown to be the executor of any bloody enterprise which he meant to commit. The Devil gave him a girdle which, being put around him, he was transformed into the likeness of a greedy, devouring wolf, strong and mighty, with eyes great and large, which in the night sparkled like brands of fire; a mouth great and wide, with most sharp and cruel teeth; a huge body and mighty paws. And no sooner would he put off the same girdle, but presently he should appear in his former shape, according to the proportion of a man, as if he had never been changed.

Stubbe Peeter herewith was exceedingly well pleased, and the shape fitted his fancy and agreed best with his nature, being inclined to blood and cruelty. Therefore, satisfied with this strange and devilish gift (for it was not troublesome but might be hidden in a small room), he proceeded to the execution of heinous and vile murders; for if any person displeased him, he would thirst for revenge, and no sooner should they or any of theirs walk in the fields or the city, but in the shape of a wolf he would presently encounter them, and never rest till he had plucked out their throats and torn their joints asunder. And after he had gotten a taste thereof, he took such pleasure and delight in shedding of blood, that he would night and day walk the fields and work extreme cruelties. And sundry times he would go through the streets of Collin, Bedbur, and Cperadt, in comely habit, and very civilly, as one well known to all the inhabitants thereabout, and often times he was saluted of those whose friends and children he had butchered, though nothing suspected for the same. In these places, I say, he would walk up and down, and if he could spy either maid, wife, or child that his eyes liked or his heart lusted after, he would wait their issuing out of the city or town. If he could by any means get

them alone, he would in the fields ravish them, and after in his wolvish likeness cruelly murder them. Often it came to pass that as he walked abroad in the fields, if he chanced to spy a company of maidens playing together or else milking their kine, in his wolvish shape he would run among them, and while the rest escaped by flight, he would be sure to lay hold of one, and after his filthy lust fulfilled, he would murder her presently. Besides, if he had liked or known any of them, her he would pursue; such was his swiftness of foot while he continued a wolf that he would outrun the swiftest greyhound in that country; and so much he had practised this wickedness that the whole province was frightened by the cruelty of this bloody and devouring wolf. Thus continuing his devilish and damnable deeds, within the compass of a few years, he had murdered thirteen young children, and two goodly young women bit with child, tearing the children out of their wombs, in most bloody and savage sort, and after ate their hearts panting hot and raw, which he accounted dainty morsels and best agreeing to his appetite.

Moreover, he used many times to kill lambs and kids and such like beasts, feeding on the same most usually raw and bloody, as if he had been a natural wolf indeed.

He had at that time living a fair young daughter, after whom he also lusted most unnaturally, and cruelly committed most wicked incest with her, a most gross and vile sin, far surmounting adultery or fornication, though the least of the three doth drive the soul into hell fire, except hearty repentance, and the great mercy of God. This daughter of his he begot when he was not altogether so wickedly given, who was called by the name of Stubbe Beell, whose beauty and good grace was such as deserved commendations of all those that knew her. And such was his inordinate lust and filthy desire toward her, that he begat a child by her, daily using her as his concubine; but as an insatiate and filthy beast, given over to work evil, with greediness he also lay by his own sister, frequenting her company long time. Moreover, being on a time sent for to a Gossip of his there to make merry and good cheer, ere he thence departed he so won the woman by

his fair and flattering speech, and so much prevailed, that ere he departed the house, he lay be
her, and ever after had her company at his
command; this woman had to name Katherine
Trompin, a woman of tall and comely stature of
exceeding good favour and one that was well
esteemed among her neighbours. But his lewd
and inordinate lust being not satisfied with the
company of many concubines, nor his wicked
fancy contented with the beauty of any
woman, at length the Devil sent unto him a
wicked spirit in the similitude and likeness of a
woman, so fair of face and comely of personage,
that she resembled rather some heavenly angel
than any mortal creature, so far her beauty
exceeded the choicest sort of women; and with
her, as with his heart's delight, he kept com-

pany the space of seven years, though in the end she proved and was found indeed no other than a she-Devil. Notwithstanding, this lewd sin of lechery did not any thing assuage his cruel and bloody mind, but continuing an insatiable bloodsucker, so great was the joy he took therein, that he accounted no day spent in pleasure wherein he had not shed some blood, not respecting so much who he did murder, as how to murder and destroy them, as the matter ensuing doth manifest, which may stand for a special note of a cruel and hard heart. For, having a proper youth to his son, begotten in the flower and strength of his age, the first fruit of his body, in whom he took such joy that he did commonly call him his heart's ease, yet so far his delight in murder

exceeded the joy he took in his son, that thirst-
ing after his blood, on a time he enticed him
into the fields, and from thence into a forest
hard by, where, making excuse to stay about the
necessaries of nature, while the young man
went forward, in the shape and likeness of a
wolf he encountered his own son and there
most cruelly slew him, which done, he presently
ate the brains out of his head as a most savory
and dainty delicious means to staunch his
greedy appetite: the most monstrous act that
ever man heard of, for never was known a
wretch from nature so far degenerate.

Long time he continued his vile and
villainous life, sometime in the likeness of a
wolf, sometime in the habit of a man, sometime in the towns and cities, and sometimes in

the woods and thickets to them adjoining, whereas the Dutch copy maketh mention; he on a time met with two men and one woman, whom he greatly desired to murder. In subtle sort he conveyed himself far before them in their way and craftily couched out of their sight; but as soon as they approached near the place where he lay, he called one of them by his name. The party, hearing himself called once or twice by his name, supposing it was some familiar friend that in jesting sort stood out of his sight, went from his company toward the place from whence the voice proceeded, of purpose to see who it was; but he was no sooner entered within the danger of this transformed man, but he was murdered in that place; the rest of his company staying for him, expecting still his return, but finding his stay over long, the other man left the woman and went to look for him, by which means the second man was also murdered. The woman then seeing neither of both return again, in heart suspected that some evil had fallen upon them, and therefore, with all the power she had, she sought to save herself by flight, though it nothing prevailed, for, good soul, she was also soon overtaken by this light-footed wolf, whom, when he had first deflowered, he after most cruelly murdered. The men were after found mangled in the wood, but the woman's body was never after seen, for she he had most ravenously devoured, whose flesh he esteemed both sweet and dainty in taste.

Thus this damnable Stubbe Peeter lived the term of five and twenty years, unsuspected to be author of so many cruel and unnatural murders, in which time he had destroyed and spoiled an unknown number of men, women, and children, sheep, lambs, and goats, and other cattle; for, when he could not through the wariness of people draw men, women, or children in his danger, then, like a cruel and tyrannous beast, he would work his cruelty on brute beasts in most savage sort, and did act more mischief and cruelty than would be credible, although high Germany hath been forced to taste the truth thereof.

By which means the inhabitants of Collin, Bedbur, and Cperadt, seeing themselves so grievously endangered, plagued, and molested by this greedy and cruel wolf, insomuch that few or none durst travel to or from those places without good provision of defence, and all for fear of this devouring and fierce wolf, for oftentimes the inhabitants found the arms and legs of dead men, women, and children scattered up and down the fields, to their great grief and vexation of heart, knowing the same to be done by that strange and cruel wolf, whom by no means they could take or overcome, so that if any man or woman missed their child, they were out of hope ever to see it alive.

And here is to be noted a most strange thing which setteth forth the great power and merciful providence of God to the comfort of each Christian heart. There were not long ago certain small children playing in a meadow together hard by the town, where also some store of kine were feeding, many of them having young calves sucking upon them. And suddenly among these children comes this vile wolf running and caught a pretty fine girl by the collar, with intent to pull out her throat; but such was the will of God, that the wolf could not pierce the collar of the child's coat, being high and very well stiffened and close clasped about her neck; and therewithal the sudden great cry of the rest of the children who escaped so amazed the cattle feeding by, that being fearful to be robbed of their young, they altogether came running against the wolf with such force that he was presently compelled to let go his hold and to run away to escape the danger of their horns; by which means the child was preserved from death, and, God be thanked, remains living at this day.

And that this thing is true, Master Tice Artine, a brewer dwelling at Puddlewharfe in London, being a man of that country born, and one of good reputation and account, is able to justify, who is near kinsman to this child, and hath from thence twice received letters concerning the same; and for that the first letter did rather drive him into wondering at the act then yielding credit thereunto, he had shortly after, at request of his writing, another letter sent to him, whereby he was more fully satisfied; and divers other persons of great credit in London hath in like sort received letters from their friends to the like effect.

Likewise in the towns of Germany aforesaid continual prayer was used unto God that it would please Him to deliver them from the danger of this greedy wolf.

And, although they had practised all the means that men could devise to take this ravenous beast, yet until the Lord had determined his fall, they could not in any wise prevail: notwithstanding they daily sought to entrap him and for that intent continually maintained great mastiffs and dogs of much strength to hunt and chase the beast. In the end, it pleased God, as they were in readiness and provided to meet with him, that they should espy him in his wolvish likeness at what time they beset him round about, and most circumspectly set their dogs upon him, in such sort that there was no means of escape, at which advantage they never could get him before; but as the Lord delivered Goliath into the hands of David, so was this wolf brought in danger of these men; who,

seeing as I said before, no way to escape the imminent danger, being hardly pursued at the heels, presently slipped his girdle from about him, whereby the shape of a wolf clean avoided, and he appeared presently in his true shape and likeness, having in his hand a staff as one walking toward the city; but the hunters, whose eyes were steadfastly bent upon the beast, and seeing him in the same place metamorphosed contrary to their expectation, it wrought a wonderful amazement to their minds; and, had it not been that they knew the man so soon as they saw him, they had surely taken the same to have been some Devil in a man's likeness; but forasmuch as they knew him to be an ancient dweller in the town, they came unto him, and talking with him, they brought him home to his own house, and finding him to be the man indeed, and no delusion or phantastical motion, they had him before the magistrates to be examined.

Thus being apprehended, he was shortly after put to the rack in the town of Bedbur, but fearing the torture, he voluntarily confessed his whole life, and made known the villainies which he had committed for the space of twenty-five years; also he confessed how by sorcery he procured of the Devil a girdle, which being put on, he forthwith became a wolf, which girdle at his apprehension he confessed he cast it off in a certain valley and there left it, which, when the magistrates heard, they sent to the valley for it, but at their coming found nothing at all, for it may be supposed it was gone to the Devil from whence it came, so that it was not to be found. For the Devil having brought the wretch to all the shame he could, left him to endure the torments which his deeds deserved.

After he had some space been imprisoned, the magistrates found out through due examination of the matter, that his daughter

Stubbe Beell and his Gossip Katherine Trompin, were both accessory to divers murders committed, were arraigned, and with Stubbe Peeter condemned, and their several judgments pronounced on the 28 of October 1589, in this manner, that is to say: Stubbe Peeter as a principal malefactor, was judged first to have his body laid on a wheel, and with red hot burning pincers in ten places to have the flesh pulled off from the bones, after that, his arms and legs and arms to be broken with a wooden axe or hatchet, afterward to have his head struck from his body, and then to have his carcase burned to ashes.

Also his daughter and his Gossip were judged to be burned quick to ashes, the same time and day with the carcase of the aforesaid

Stubbe Peeter. And on the 31st of the same month, they suffered death accordingly in the town of Bedbur in the presence of many peers and princes of Germany.

Thus, Gentle Reader, have I set down the true discourse of this wicked man Stubbe Peeter, which I desire to be a warning to all sorcerers and witches, which unlawfully follow their own devilish imagination to the utter ruin and destruction of their souls eternally, from which wicked and damnable practice, I beseech God keep all good men, and from the cruelty of their wicked hearts. Amen.

After the execution, there was by the advice of the magistrates of the town of Bedbur a high pole set up and strongly framed, which first went through the wheel whereon he was broken, whereunto also it was fastened; after that a little above the wheel the likeness of a wolf was framed in wood, to show unto all men the shape wherein he executed those cruelties. Over that on the top of the stake the sorcerer's head itself was set up, and round about the wheel there hunt as it were sixteen pieces of wood about a yard in length which represented the sixteen persons that were perfectly known to be murdered by him. And the same ordained to stand there for a continual monument to all ensuing ages, what murders by Stubbe Peeter were committed, with the order of his judgement, as this picture doth more plainly express.

Witnesses that this is true: Tyse Artyne, William Brewar, Adolf Staedt, George Bores. With divers others that have seen the same.

GABRIEL-ERNEST

THERE IS A wild beast in your woods," said the artist Cunningham, as he was being driven to the station. It was the only remark he had made during the drive, but as Van Cheele had talked incessantly his companion's silence had not been noticeable.

"A stray fox or two and some resident weasels. Nothing more formidable," said Van Cheele. The artist said nothing.

"What did you mean about a wild beast?" said Van Cheele later, when they were on the platform.

"Nothing. My imagination. Here is the train," said Cunningham.

That afternoon Van Cheele went for one of his frequent rambles through his woodland property. He had a stuffed bittern in his study, and knew the names of quite a number of wild flowers, so his aunt had possibly some justification in describing him as a great naturalist. At any rate, he was a great walker. It was his custom to take mental notes of everything he saw during his walks, not so much for the purpose of assisting contemporary science as to provide topics for conversation afterwards. When the bluebells began to show themselves in flower he made a point of informing everyone of the fact; the season of the year might have warned his hearers of the likelihood of such an occurrence, but at least they felt that he was being absolutely frank with them.

What Van Cheele saw on this particular afternoon was, however, something far removed from his ordinary range of experience. On a shelf of smooth stone overhanging a deep pool in the hollow of an oak coppice a boy of about sixteen lay asprawl, drying his wet brown limbs luxuriously in the sun. His wet hair, parted by a recent dive, lay close to his head, and his light-brown eyes, so light that there was an almost tigerish gleam in them, were turned towards Van Cheele with a certain lazy watchfulness. It was an unexected apparition, and Van Cheele found himself engaged in the novel process of thinking before he spoke. Where on earth could this wild-looking boy hail from? The miller's wife had lost a child some two months ago, supposed to have been swept away by the mill-race, but that had been a mere baby, not a half-grown lad.

"What are you doing there?" he

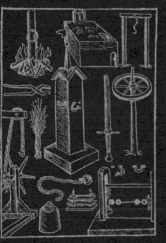

demanded.

"Obviously, sunning myself," replied the boy.

"Where do you live?"

"Here, in these woods."

"You can't live

in the woods," said Van Cheele.

"They are very nice woods," said the boy, with a touch of patronage in his voice.

"But where do you sleep at night?"

"I don't sleep at night; that's my busiest time."

Van Cheele began to have an irritated feeling that he was grappling with a problem that was eluding him.

"What do you feed on?" he asked.

"Flesh," said the boy, and he pronounced the word with slow relish, as though he were tasting it.

"Flesh! What flesh?"

"Since it interests you, rabbits, wild-fowl, hares, poultry, lambs in their season, children when I can get any; they're usually oo well locked in at night, which I do most of my hunting. It's quite two months since I tasted child-flesh."

Ignoring the chaffing nature of the last remark, Van Cheele tried to draw the boy on the subject of possible poaching operations.

"You're talking rather through your hat when you speak of feeding on hares." (Considering the nature of the boy's toilet, the simile was hardly an apt one.) "Our hillside hares aren't easily caught."

"At night I hunt on four feet," was the somewhat cryptic response.

"I suppose you mean that you hunt with a dog?" hazarded Van Cheele.

The boy rolled slowly over on to his

back, and laughed a weird low laugh, that was pleasantly like a chuckle and disagreeably like a snarl.

"I don't fancy any dog would be very anxious for my company, especially at night."

Van Cheele began to feel that there was something positively uncanny about the strange-eyed, strange-tongued youngster.

"I can't have you staying in these woods," he declared authoritatively.

"I fancy you'd rather have me here than in your house," said the boy.

The prospect of this wild, nude animal in Van Cheele's primly ordered house was certainly an alarming one.

"If you don't go, I shall have to make you," said Van Cheele.

The boy turned like a flash, plunged into the pool, and in a moment had flung his wet and glistening body halfway up the bank where Van Cheele was standing. In an otter the movement would not have been remarkable; in a boy Van Cheele found it sufficiently startling. His foot slipped as he made an involuntary backward movement, and he found himself almost prostrate on the slippery weed-grown bank, with those tigerish yellow eyes not very far from his own. Almost instinctively he half raised his hand to his throat. The boy laughed again, a laugh in which the snarl had nearly driven out the chuckle, and then, with another of his astonishing lightning movements, plunged out of view into a yielding tangle of weed and fern.

"What an extraordinary wild animal!" said Van Cheele as he picked himself up. And then he recalled Cunningham's remark, "There is a wild beast in your woods."

Walking slowly homeward, Van Cheele began to turn over in his mind various local occurrences which might be traceable to the existence of this astonishing young savage.

Something had been thinning the game in the woods lately, poultry had been missing from the farms, hares were growing unaccountably scarcer, and complaints had reached him of lambs being carried off bodily from the hills. Was it possible that this wild boy was really hunting the countryside in companion with some clever poacher dog?

He had spoken of hunting "four-footed" by night, but then, again, he had hinted strangely at no dog caring to come near him, "especially at night." It was certainly puzzling. And then, as Van Cheele ran his mind over the various depredations that had been committed during the last month or two, he came suddenly to a dead stop, alike in his walk and his speculations. The child missing from the mill two months ago—the accepted theory was that it had tumbled into the mill-race and been swept away; but the mother had always declared she had heard a shriek on the hill side of the house, in the opposite direction from the water. It was unthinkable, of course, but he wished that the boy had not made that uncanny remark about child-flesh eaten two months ago. Such dreadful things should not be said even in fun.

Van Cheele, contrary to his usual wont, did not feel disposed to be communicative about his discovery in the wood. His position as a parish councillor and justice of the peace seemed somehow comprised by the fact that he was harboring a personality of such doubtful repute on his property; there was even a possibility that a heavy bill of damages for raided lambs and poultry might be laid at his door. At dinner that night he was quite unusually silent.

"Where's your voice gone to?" said his aunt. "One would think you had seen a wolf."

Van Cheele, who was not familiar with the old saying, thought the remark rather foolish; if he *had* seen a wolf on his property his tongue would have been extraordinarily busy with the subject.

At breakfast next morning Van Cheele was conscious that his feeling of uneasiness regarding yesterday's episode had not wholly disappeared, and he resolved to go by train to the neighboring cathedral town, hunt up Cunningham, and learn from him what he had really seen that had prompted the remark about a wild beast in the woods. With this resolution taken, his usual cheerfulness partially returned, and he hummed a bright little melody as he sauntered to the morning room for his customary cigarette. As he entered the room the melody made way abruptly for a pious invocation. Gracefully asprawl on the ottoman, in an attitude of almost exaggerated repose, was the boy of the woods. He was drier than when Van Cheele had last seen him, but no other alteration was noticeable in his toilet.

"How dare you come here?" asked Van Cheele furiously.

"You told me I was not to stay in the woods," said the boy calmly.

"But not to come here. Supposing my aunt should see you!"

And with a view to minimizing that catastrophe Van Cheele hastily obscured as much of his unwelcome guest as possible under the folds of a *Morning Post*. At that moment his aunt entered the room.

"This a poor boy who has lost his way—and lost his memory. He doesn't know who he is or where he comes from," explained Van Cheele desperately, glancing apprehensively at the waif's face to see whether he was going to add inconvenient candor to his other savage propensities.

Miss Van Cheele was enormously interested.

"Perhaps his underlinen is marked," she suggested.

"He seems to have lost most of that, too," said Van Cheele, making frantic little grabs at the *Morning Post* to keep it in its place.

A naked, homeless child appealed to Miss Van Cheele as warmly as a stray kitten or derelict puppy would have done.

"We must do all we can for him," she decided, and in a very short time a messenger, dispatched to the rectory, where a page-boy was kept, had returned with a suit of pantry clothes, and the necessary accessories of shirt, shoes, collar, etc. Clothed, clean and groomed, the boy lost none of his uncanniness in Van Cheele's eyes, but his aunt found him sweet.

"We must call him something till we know who he really is," she said. "Gabriel-Ernest, I think; those are nice suitable names."

Van Cheele agreed, but he privately doubted whether they were being grafted on to a nice suitable child. His misgivings were not diminished by the fact that his staid and elderly spaniel had bolted out of the house at the first incoming of the boy, and now obstinately remained shivering and yapping at the farther end of the orchard, while the canary, usually as vocally industrious as Van Cheele himself, had put itself on an allowance of frightened cheeps. More than ever he was resolved to consult Cunningham without loss of time.

As he drove off to the station his aunt was arranging that Gabriel-Ernest should help her to entertain the infant members of her Sunday-school class at tea that afternoon.

Cunningham was not at first disposed to be communicative.

"My mother died of some brain trouble," he explained, "so you will understand why I am averse to dwelling on anything of an impossibly fantastic nature that I may see or think that I have seen."

"But what *did* you see?" persisted Van Cheele.

"What I thought I saw was something so extraordinary that no really sane man could dignify it with the credit of having actually happened. I was standing, the last evening I was with you, half-hidden in the hedgegrowth by the orchard gate, watching the dying glow of the sunset. Suddenly I became aware of a naked boy, a bather from some neighboring pool, I took him to be, who was standing out on the bare hillside also watching the sunset. His pose was so suggestive of some wild faun of Pagan myth that I instantly wanted to engage him as a model, and in another moment I think I should have hailed him. But just then the sun dipped out of view, and all the orange and pink slid out of the landscape, leaving it cold and gray. And at the same moment an astounding thing happened—the boy vanished too!"

"What! Vanished away into nothing?" asked Van Cheele excitedly.

"No; that is the dreadful part of it," answered the artist; "on the open hillside where the boy had been standing a second ago, stood a large wolf, blackish in color, with gleaming fangs and cruel, yellow eyes. You may think—"

But Van Cheele did not stop for anything as futile as thought. Already he was tearing at top speed towards the station. He dismissed the idea of a telegram. "Gabriel-Ernest is a werewolf" was a hopelessly inadequate effort at conveying the situation, and his aunt would think it was a code message to which he had omitted to give her the key. His one hope was that he might reach home before sundown. The cab which he chartered at the other end of the railway journey bore him with what seemed exasperating slowness along the country roads, which were pink and mauve with the flush of the sinking sun. His aunt was putting away some unfinished jams and cake when he arrived.

"Where is Gabriel-Ernest?" he almost screamed.

"He is taking the little Toop child home," said his aunt. "It was getting so late, I thought it wasn't safe to let it go back alone. What a lovely sunset, isn't it?"

But Van Cheele, although not oblivious of the glow in the western sky, did not stay to discuss its beauties. At a speed for which he was scarcely geared he raced along the narrow lane that led to the home of the Toops. On one side ran the swift current of the mill-stream, on the other rose the stretch of bare hillside. A dwindling rim of red sun showed still on the skyline, and the next turning must bring him in view of the ill-assorted couple he was pursuing. Then the color went suddenly out of things, and a gray light settled itself with a quick shiver over the landscape. Van Cheele heard a shrill wail of fear, and stopped running.

Nothing was ever seen again of the Toops' child or Gabriel-Ernest, but the latter's discarded garments were found lying in the road, so it was assumed that the child had fallen into the water, and that the boy had stripped and jumped in, in a vain endeavor to save it. Van Cheele and some workmen who were nearby at the time testified to having heard a child scream loudly just near the spot where the clothes were found. Mrs. Toop, who had eleven other children, was decently resigned to her bereavement, but Miss Van Cheele sincerely mourned her lost foundling. It was on her initiative that a memorial brass was put up in the parish church to "Gabriel-Ernest, an unknown boy, who bravely sacrificed his life for another."

Van Cheele gave way to his aunt in most things, but he flatly refused to subscribe to the Gabriel-Ernest memorial.

CHARMS AND SPELLS

SPIRITS FROM THE deep
Who never sleep,
  Be kind to me.

Spirits from the grave
Without a soul to save,
  Be kind to me.

Spirits of the trees
That grow upon the leas,
  Be kind to me.

Spirits of the air,
Foul and black, not fair,
    Be kind to me.

Water spirits hateful,
To ships and bathers fateful,
    Be kind to me.

Spirits of earthbound dead
That glide with noiseless tread,
       Be kind to me.

Spirits of heat and fire,
Destructive in your ire,
       Be kind to me.

Spirits of cold and ice,
Patrons of crime and vice,
       Be kind to me.

Wolves, vampires, satyrs, ghosts!
Elect of all the devilish hosts!
I pray you send hither,
       Send hither, send hither,
The great gray shape that makes men shiver!

Shiver, shiver, shiver!
> Come! Come! Come!

Come, spirit so powerful! Come, spirit so dread,
From the home of the werewolf, the home of
the dead.
Come, give me thy blessing! Come, lend me
thine ear!
Oh spirit of darkness! Oh spirit so drear!

Come, mighty phantom! Come, great Unknown!
Come from thy dwelling so gloomy and lone.
Come, I beseech thee; depart from thy lair,
And body and soul shall be thine, I declare.

Haste, haste, haste, horrid spirit, haste!
Speed, speed, speed, scaring spirit, speed!
Fast, fast, fast, fateful spirit, fast!

I offer to thee, Great Spirit of the Unknown, this
night, my body and soul, on condition that thou
grantest me, from this night to the hour of my
death, the power of metamorphosing, nocturnally,
into a wolf. I beg, I pray, I implore thee—thee,
unparalleled Phantom of Darkness, to make me a
werewolf—a werewolf!

Make me a werewolf! Make me a man-eater!
Make me a werewolf! Make me a woman-eater!
Make me a werewolf! Make me a child-eater!
I pine for blood! Human blood!
Give it me! Give it me tonight!
Great Wolf Spirit! Give it me, and
Heart, body, and soul, I am yours.

Tis night! 'Tis night! And the moon shines white
          Over pine and snow-capped hill;

The shadows stray through burn and brae
        And dance in the sparkling rill.

'Tis night! 'Tis night! And the devil's light
        Casts glimmering beams around.
The maras dance, the nisses prance
        On the flower-enamelled ground.
'Tis night! 'Tis night! And the werewolf's might
        Makes men and nature shiver.
Yet its fierce gray head and stealthy tread
        Are nought to thee, oh river!
River, river, river.
Oh water strong, that swirls along,
        I prithee a werewolf make me.
Of all things dear, my soul, I swear,
        In death shall not forsake thee.

A Treatise

WOLF-MADNESS, IS a disease, in which men run barking and howling about graves and fields in the night, lying hid for the most part all day, and will not be persuaded but that they are Wolves, or some such beasts.

. . . they have usually hollow eyes, scabbed legs and thighs, very dry and pale. . . .

A certain young man, in this City, tall, slender, and black, of a wild and strange look, was taken with this kind of malady, for he run barking and howling about the room where he was. . . . I remember I opened a vein, and drew forth a very large quantity of blood, black like Soot; after which, I gave him this Potion. . . . And lastly I gave him this vomit. . . . This wrought upward and downward; after which he became perfectly well.

BRAM STOKER

Dracula's Guest

WHEN WE STARTED for our drive the sun was shining brightly on Munich, and the air was full of the joyousness of early summer. Just as we were about to depart, Herr Delbrück (the maître d'hôtel of the Quatre Saisons, where I was staying) came down, bareheaded, to the carriage and, after wishing me a pleasant drive, said to the coachman, still holding his hand on the handle of the carriage door:

"Remember you are back by nightfall. The sky looks bright but there is a shiver in the north wind that says there may be a sudden storm. But I am sure you will not be late." Here he smiled, and added, "for you know what night it is."

Johann answered with an emphatic, "Ja, mein Herr," and, touching his hat, drove off quickly. When we had cleared the town, I said, after signalling to him to stop:

"Tell me, Johann, what is tonight?"

He crossed himself, as he answered laconically: "Walpurgis Nacht." Then he took out his watch, a great, old-fashioned German silver thing as big as a turnip, and looked at it, with his eyebrows gathered together and a little impatient shrug of his shoulders. I realized that this was his way of respectfully protesting against the unnecessary delay, and sank back in the carriage, merely motioning him to proceed. He started off rapidly, as if to make up for lost time. Every now and then the horses seemed to throw up their heads and sniffed the air suspiciously. On such occasions I often looked round in alarm. The road was pretty bleak, for we were traversing a sort of high, wind-swept plateau. As we drove, I saw a road that looked but little used, and which seemed to dip through a little, winding valley. It looked so inviting that, even at the risk of offending him, I called Johann to stop—and when he had pulled up, I told him I would like to drive down that road. He made all sorts of excuses, and frequently crossed himself as he spoke. This somewhat piqued my curiosity, so I asked him various questions. He answered fencingly, and repeatedly looked at his watch in protest. Finally I said:

"Well, Johann, I want to go down this road. I shall not ask you to come unless you like; but tell me why you do not like to go, that is all I ask." For answer he seemed to throw himself off the box, so quickly did he reach the ground. Then he stretched out his hands appealingly to me, and implored me not to go. There was just enough of English mixed with the German for me to understand the drift of his talk. He seemed always just about to tell me something—the very idea of which evidently frightened him; but each time he pulled himself up, saying, as he crossed himself: "Walpurgis Nacht!"

I tried to argue with him, but it was difficult to argue with a man when I did not know his language. The advantage certainly rested with him, for although he began to speak in English, of a very crude and broken kind, he always got excited and broke into his native tongue—and every time he did so, he looked at his watch. Then the horses became restless and sniffed the air. At this he grew very pale, and, looking around in a frightened way, he suddenly jumped forward, took them by the bridles and led them on some twenty feet. I followed, and asked why he had done this. For answer he crossed himself, pointed to the spot

we had left and drew his carriage in the direction of the other road, indicating a cross, and said, first in German, then in English: "Buried him—him what killed themselves."

I remembered the old custom of burying suicides at cross-roads: "Ah! I see, a suicide. How interesting!" But for the life of me I could not make out why the horses were frightened.

Whilst we were talking, we heard a sort of sound between a yelp and a bark. It was far away; but the horses got very restless, and it took Johann all his time to quiet them. He was pale, and said, "It sounds like a wolf—but yet there are no wolves here now."

"No?" I said, questioning him; "isn't it long since the wolves were so near the city?"

"Long, long," he answered, "in the spring and summer; but with the snow the wolves have been here not so long."

Whilst he was petting the horses and trying to quiet them, dark clouds drifted rapidly across the sky. The sunshine passed away, and a breath of cold wind seemed to drift past us. It was only a breath, however, and more in the nature of a warning than a fact, for the sun came out brightly again. Johann looked under his lifted hand at the horizon and said:

"The storm of snow, he comes before long time." Then he looked at his watch again, and, straightaway holding his reins firmly—for the horses were still pawing the ground restlessly and shaking their heads— he climbed to his box as though the time had come for proceeding on our journey.

I felt a little obstinate and did not at once get into the carriage.

"Tell me," I said, "about this place where the road leads," and I pointed down.

Again he crossed himself and mumbled a prayer, before he answered, "It is unholy."

"What is unholy?" I enquired.

"The village."

"Then there is a village?"

"No, no. No one lives there hundreds of years." My curiosity was piqued. "But you said there was a village."

"There was."

"Where is it now?"

Whereupon he burst out into a long story in German and English, so mixed up that I could not quite understand exactly what he said, but roughly I gathered that long ago, hundreds of years, men had died there and been buried in their graves; and sounds were heard under the clay, and when the graves were opened, men and women were found rosy with life, and their mouths red with blood. And so, in haste to save their lives (aye, and their souls!—and here he crossed himself) those who were left fled away to other places, where the living lived, and the dead were dead and not—not something. He was evidently afraid to speak the last words. As he proceeded with his narration, he grew more and more excited. It seemed as if his imagination had got hold of him, and he ended in a perfect paroxysm of fear—white-faced, perspiring, trembling and looking round him, as if expecting that some dreadful presence would manifest itself there in the bright sunshine on the open plain. Finally, in an agony of desperation, he cried:

"Walpurgis Nacht!" and pointed to the carriage for me to get in. All my English blood rose at this, and, standing back, I said:

"You are afraid, Johann—you are afraid. Go home; I shall return alone; the walk will do me good." The carriage door was open. I took from my seat my oak walking stick—which I always carry on my holiday excursions—and closed the door, pointing back to Munich, and said, "Go home, Johann—Walpurgis Nacht doesn't concern Englishmen."

The horses were now more restive than ever, and Johann was trying to hold them in, while excitedly imploring me not to do anything so foolish. I pitied the poor fellow, he was deeply in earnest; but all the same I could not help laughing. His English was quite gone now. In his anxiety he had forgot-

ten that his only means of making me understand was to talk my language, so he jabbered
away in his native German. It began to be a
little tedious. After giving the direction,
"Home!" I turned to go down the cross-road
into the valley.

With a despairing gesture, Johann
turned his horses towards Munich. I leaned on
my stick and looked after him. He went
slowly along the road for a while: then there
came over the crest of the hill a man tall and
thin. I could see so much in the distance.
When he drew near the horses, they began to
jump and kick about, then to scream with terror. Johann could not hold them in; they
bolted down the road, running away madly. I
watched them out of sight, then looked for the

stranger, but I found that he, too, was gone.

With a light heart I turned down the side road through the deepening valley to which Johann had objected. There was not the slightest reason, that I could see, for his objection; and I daresay I tramped for a couple of hours without thinking of time or distance, and certainly without seeing a person or a house. So far as the place was concerned, it was desolation itself. But I did not notice this particularly till, on turning a bend in the road, I came upon a scattered fringe of wood; then I recognized that I had been impressed unconsciously by the desolation of the region through which I had passed.

I sat down to rest myself, and began to look around. It struck me that it was consid-

erably colder than it had been at the com-
mencement of my walk—a sort of sighing
sound seemed to be around me, with, now
and then, high overhead, a sort of muffled
roar. Looking upwards I noticed that great
thick clouds were drifting rapidly across the
sky from north to south at a great height.
There were signs of coming storm in some
lofty stratum of the air. I was a little chilly,
and, thinking that it was the sitting still after
the exercise of walking, I resumed my journey.

The ground I passed over was now
much more picturesque. There were no strik-
ing objects that the eye might single out; but
in all there was a charm of beauty. I took little
heed of time and it was only when the deepening twilight forced itself upon me that I

began to think about how I should find my way home. The brightness of the day had gone. The air was cold, and the drifting of clouds high overhead was more marked. They were accompanied by a sort of far-away rushing sound, through which seemed to come at intervals that mysterious cry which the driver had said came from a wolf. For a while I hesitated. I had said I would see the deserted village, so on I went, and presently came on a wide stretch of open country, shut in by hills all around. Their sides were covered with trees which spread down to the plain, dotting, in clumps, the gentler slopes and hollows which showed here and there. I followed with my eye the winding of the road, and saw that it curved close to one of the densest of these clumps and was lost behind it.

As I looked there came a cold shiver in the air, and the snow began to fall. I thought of the miles and miles of bleak country I had passed, and then hurried on to seek the shelter of the wood in front. Darker and darker grew the sky, and faster and heavier fell the snow, till the earth before and around me was a glistening white carpet the further edge of which was lost in misty vagueness. The road was here but crude, and when on the level its boundaries were not so marked, as when it passed through the cuttings; and in a little while I found that I must have strayed from it, for I missed underfoot the hard surface, and my feet sank deeper in the grass and moss. Then the wind grew stronger and blew with ever-increasing force, till I was fain to run before it. The air became icy-cold, and in spite of my exercise I began to suffer. The snow  was now falling so thickly and whirling around me in such rapid eddies that I could hardly keep my eyes open. Every now and then the heavens were torn asunder by vivid lightning, and in the flashes I could see ahead of me a great mass of trees, chiefly yew and cypress all heavily coated with snow.

I was soon amongst the shelter of the trees, and there, in comparative silence, I could hear the rush of the wind high overhead. Presently the blackness of the storm had become merged in the darkness of the night. By-and-by the storm seemed to be passing away: it now only came in fierce puffs or blasts. At such moments the weird sound of the wolf appeared to be echoed by many similar sounds around me.

Now and again, through the black mass of drifting cloud, came a straggling ray of moonlight, which lit up the expanse, and showed me that I was at the edge of a dense mass of cypress and yew trees. As the snow had ceased to fall, I walked out from the shelter and began to investigate more closely. It appeared to me that, amongst so many old foundations as I had passed, there might be still standing a house which, though in ruins, I could find some sort of shelter for a while. As I skirted the edge of the corpse, I found that a low wall encircled it, and following this I presently found an opening. Here the cypresses formed an alley leading up to a square mass of some kind of building. Just as I caught sight of this, however, the drifting clouds obscured the moon, and I passed up the path in darkness. The wind must have grown colder, for I felt myself shiver as I walked; but there was hope of shelter, and I groped my way blindly on.

I stopped, for there was a sudden stillness. The storm had passed; and, perhaps in sympathy with nature's silence, my heart seemed to cease to beat. But this was only momentarily; for suddenly the moonlight broke through the clouds, showing me that I was in a graveyard, and that the square object before me was a great massive tomb of marble, as white as the snow that lay on and all around it. With the moonlight there came a fierce sigh of the storm, which appeared to resume its course with a long, low howl, as of many dogs of wolves. I was awed and shocked, and felt the cold perceptibly grow upon me till it seemed to grip me by the heart. Then while the flood of moonlight still fell on the marble tomb, the storm gave further evidence of renewing, as though it was returning on its track. Impelled by some sort of fascination, I approached the sepulchre to see what it was, and why such a thing stood alone in such a place. I walked around it, and read, over the Doric door, in German:

COUNTESS DOLINGEN OF GRATZ

IN STYRIA

SOUGHT AND FOUND DEATH

1801

On the top of the tomb, seemingly driven through the solid marble—for the structure was composed of a few vast blocks of stone—was a great iron spike or stake. On going to the back I saw, graven in great Russian letters:

The dead travel fast.

There was something so weird and uncanny about the whole thing that it gave me a turn and made me feel quite faint. I began to wish, for the first time, that I had taken Johann's advice. Here a thought struck me, which came under almost mysterious circumstances and with a terrible shock. This was Walpurgis Night!

Walpurgis Night, when, according to the belief of millions of people, the devil was abroad—when the graves were opened and the dead came forth and walked. When all evil things of earth and air and water held revel. This very place the driver had specially shunned. This was the depopulated village of centuries ago. This was where the suicide lay; and this was the place where I was alone—

unmanned, shivering with cold in a shroud of snow with a wild storm gathering again upon me! It took all my philosophy, all the religion I had been taught, all my courage, not to collapse in a paroxysm of fright.

And now a perfect tornado burst upon me. The ground shook as though thousands of horses thundered across it; and this time the storm bore on its icy wings, not snow, but great hailstones which drove with such violence that they might have come from the thongs of Balearic slingers—hailstones that beat down leaf and branch and made the shelter of the cypresses of no more avail than though their stems were standing-corn. At the first I had rushed to the nearest tree; but I was soon fain to leave it and seek the only spot that seemed to afford refuge, the deep Doric doorway of the marble tomb. There, crouching against the massive bronze door, I gained a certain amount of protection from the beating of the hailstones, for now they only drove against me as they ricocheted from the ground and the side of the marble.

As I leaned against the door, it moved slightly and opened inwards. The shelter of even a tomb was welcome in that pitiless tempest, and I was about to enter it when there came a flash of forked-lightning that lit up the whole expanse of the heavens. In the instant, as I am a living man, I saw, as my eyes were turned into the darkness of the tomb, a beautiful woman, with rounded cheeks and red lips, seemingly sleeping on a bier. As the thunder broke overhead, I was grasped as by the hand of a giant and hurled out into the storm. The whole thing was so sudden that, before I could realize the shock, moral as well as physical, I found the hailstones beating me down. At the same time I had a strange dominating feeling that I was not alone. I looked towards the tomb. Just then there came another blinding flash, which seemed to strike the iron stake that surmounted the tomb and to pour through to the earth, blasting and crumbling the marble, as in a burst of flame. The dead woman rose for a moment of agony, while she was lapped in the flame, and her bitter scream of pain was drowned in the thundercrash. The last thing I heard was this mingling of dreadful sound, as again I was seized in the giant-grasp and dragged away, while the hailstones beat on me, and the air around seemed reverberant with the howling of wolves. The last sight that I remembered was a vague, white, moving mass, as if all the graves around me had sent out the phantoms of their sheeted dead, and that they were closing in on me through the white cloudiness of the driving hail.

GRADUALLY THERE CAME a sort of vague beginning of consciousness; then a sense of weariness that was dreadful. For a time I remembered nothing; but slowly my senses returned. My feet seemed positively racked with pain, yet I could not move them. They seemed to be numbed. There was an icy feeling at the back of my neck and all down my spine, and my ears, like my feet, were dead, yet in torment; but there was in my breast a sense of warmth which was, by comparison, delicious. It was as a nightmare—a physical nightmare, if one may use such an expression; for some heavy weight on my chest made it difficult for me to breathe.

This period of semi-lethargy seemed to remain a long time, and as it faded away I must have slept or swooned. Then came a sort of loathing, like the first stage of seasickness, and a wild desire to be free from something— I knew not what. A vast stillness enveloped me, as though all the world were asleep or dead—only broken by the low panting as of some animal close to me. I felt a warm rasping at my throat, then came a consciousness of the awful truth, which chilled me to the heart and sent the blood surging up through my brain. Some great animal was lying on me and now licking my throat. I feared to stir, for some instinct of prudence bade me lie still; but the brute seemed to realize that there was now some change in me, for it raised its head. Through my eyelashes I saw above me the two great flaming eyes of a gigantic wolf. Its sharp white teeth gleamed in the gaping red mouth, and I could feel its hot breath fierce and acrid upon me.

For another spell of time I remembered no more. Then I became conscious of a low growl, followed by a yelp, renewed again and again. Then, seemingly very far away, I

heard a "Holloa! holloa!" as of many voices
calling in unison. Cautiously I raised my head
and looked in the direction whence the
sound came; but the cemetery blocked my
view. The wolf still continued to yelp in a
strange way and a red glare began to move
round the grove of the cypresses, as though
following the sound. As the voices drew
closer, the wolf yelped faster and louder. I
feared to make either sound or motion.
Nearer came the red glow, over the white pall
which stretched into the darkness around me.
Then all at once from beyond the trees there
came at a trot a troop of horsemen bearing
torches. The wolf rose from my breast and
made for the cemetery. I saw one of the horsemen (soldiers by their caps and their long mil-

itary cloaks) raise his carbine and take aim. A companion knocked up his arm, and I heard the ball whizz over my head. He had evidently taken my body for that of the wolf. Another sighted the animal as it slunk away, and a shot followed. Then, at a gallop, the troop rode forward—some towards me, others following the wolf as it disappeared amongst the snow-clad cypresses.

As they drew nearer I tried to move, but was powerless, although I could see and hear all that went on around me. Two or three of the soldiers jumped from their horses and knelt beside me. One of them raised my head, and placed his hand over my heart.

"Good news, comrades!" he cried. "His heart still beats!"

Then some brandy was poured down my throat; it put vigor into me, and I was able to open my eyes fully and look around. Lights and shadows were moving among the trees, and I heard men call to one another. They drew together, uttering frightened exclamations; and the lights flashed as the others came pouring out of the cemetery pell-mell, like men possessed. When the further ones came close to us, those who were around me asked them eagerly:

"Well, have you found him?"

The reply rang out hurriedly:

"No! no! Come away quick—quick! This is no place to stay, and on this of all nights!"

"What was it?" was the question, asked in a manner of keys. The answer came variously and all indefinitely as though the men were moved by some common impulse to speak, yet were restrained by some common fear from giving their thoughts.

"It—it—indeed!" gibbered one, whose wits had plainly given out for the moment.

"A wolf—and yet not a wolf!" another put it shudderingly.

"No use trying for him without the sacred bullet," a third remarked in a more ordinary manner.

"Serve us right for coming out on this night! Truly we have earned our thousand marks!" were the ejaculations of a fourth.

"There was blood on the broken marble," another said after a pause—"the lightning never brought that there. And for him—is he safe? Look at his throat! See, comrades, the wolf has been lying on him and keeping his blood warm."

The officer looked at my throat and replied:

"He is all right; the skin is not pierced. What does it all mean? We should never have found him but for the yelping of the wolf."

"What became of it?" asked the man who was holding up my head, and who seemed the least panic-stricken of the party, for his hands were steady and without tremor. On his sleeve was the chevron of a petty officer.

"It went to its home," answered the man, whose long face was pallid, and who actually shook with terror as he glanced around him

fearfully. "There are graves enough there in which it may lie. Come, comrades—come quickly! Let us leave this cursed spot."

The officer raised me to a sitting posture, as he uttered a word of command; then several men placed me upon a horse. He sprang to the saddle behind me, took me in his arms, gave the word to advance; and, turning our faces away from the cypresses, we rode away in swift military order.

As yet my tongue refused its office, and I was perforce silent. I must have fallen asleep; for the next thing I remember was finding myself standing up, supported by a soldier on each side of me. It was almost broad daylight, and to the north a red streak of sunlight was reflected, like a path of blood, over the waste of snow. The officer was telling the men to say nothing of what they had seen, except that they found an English stranger, guarded by a large dog.

"Dog! that was no dog," cut in the man who had exhibited such fear. "I think I know a wolf when I see one."

The young officer answered calmly:

"I said a dog."

"Dog!" reiterated the other ironically. It was evident that his courage was rising with the sun; and, pointing to me, he said, "Look at his throat. Is that the work of a dog, master?"

Instinctively I raised my hand to my throat, and as I touched it I cried out in pain. The men crowded round to look, some stooping down from their saddles; and again there came the calm voice of the young officer:

"A dog, as I said. If aught else were said we should only be laughed at."

I was then mounted behind a trooper, and we rode on into the suburbs of Munich. Here we came across a stray carriage, into which I was lifted, and it was driven off to the

Quatre Saisons—the young officer accompanying me, whilst a trooper followed with his horse, and the others rode off to their barracks.

When we arrived, Herr Delbrück rushed so quickly down the steps to meet me, that it was apparent he had been watching within. Taking me by both hands he solicitously led me in. The officer saluted me and was turning to withdraw, when I recognized his purpose, and insisted that he should come to my rooms. Over a glass of wine I warmly thanked him and his brave comrades for saving me. He replied simply that he was more than glad, and that Herr Delbrück had at the first taken steps to make all the searching party pleased; at which ambiguous utterance the maître d'hôtel smiled, while the officer pleaded duty and withdrew.

"But Herr Delbrück," I enquired, "how and why was it that the soldiers searched for me?"

He shrugged his shoulders, as if in depreciation of his own deed, as he replied:

"I was so fortunate as to obtain leave from the commander of the regiment in which I served, to ask for volunteers."

"But how did you know I was lost?" I asked.

"The driver came hither with the remains of his carriage, which had been upset when the horses ran away."

"But surely you would not send a search party of soldiers merely on this account?"

"Oh, no!" he answered; "but even before the coachman arrived, I had this telegram from the Boyar whose guest you are," and he took from his pocket a telegram which he handed to me, and I read:

Bistritz.

Be careful of my guest—his safety is most precious to me. Should aught happen to him, or if he be missed, spare nothing to find him and ensure his safety. He is English and therefore adventurous. There are often dangers from snow and wolves and night. Lose not a moment if you suspect harm to him. I answer your zeal with my fortune. —*Dracula.*

As I HELD the telegram in my hand, the room seemed to whirl around me; and, if the attentive maître d'hôtel had not caught me, I think I should have fallen. There was something so strange in all this, something so weird and impossible to imagine, that there grew on me a sense of my being in some way the sport of opposite forces—the mere vague idea of which seemed in a way to paralyze me. I was certainly under some form of mysterious protection. From a distant country had come, in the very nick of time, a message that took me out of the danger of the snow-sleep and the jaws of the wolf.

THE
SATYRICON

AFTER THIS, WHEN all of us had wished him Health and Happiness, Trimalchio, turning to Niceros, "You were wont," said he, "to be a good Companion, but what's the matter we get not a word from ye now? Let me entreat ye, as you would see me Happy, do not break an old Custom."

Niceros, please with the frankness of his Friend: "Let me never thrive," said he, "if

I am not ready to caper out of my Skin, to see you in so good a Humour; therefore what I say shall be all Mirth; tho' I am afraid those Grave Fopps may laugh: but let them look to 't, I'll go on nevertheless; for what am I the worse for any one Swearing? I had rather they laugh at what I say, than at my self."

Thus when he spake— —he began this Tale:—

"While I was yet a Servant we liv'd in a narrow Lane, now the House of Gavilla: There, as the Gods would have it, I fell in Love with Tarentius's Wife; he kept an Eating-house. Ye all knew Melissa Tarentina, a pretty little Punching-block, and withal Beautiful; but (so help me Hercules) I minded her not so much for the matter of the point of that, as that she was good-humour'd; if I asked her any thing, she never deny'd me; and what Money I had, I trusted her with it; nor did she ever fail me when I'd occasion. It so happened, that a she-companion of hers had dy'd in the Country, and she was gone thither; how to come at her I could not tell; but a Friend is seen at a dead lift; it also happened my Master was gone to Capua to dispatch somewhat or other: I laid hold of the opportunity, and persuaded mine Host to take an Evenings Walk of four or five Miles out of Town, for he was a stout Fellow, and as bold as a Devil: The Moon shone as bright as Day, and about Cockcrowing we fell in with a Bury-ing-place, and certain Monuments of the Dead: my Man loitered behind me a star-gazing, and I sitting expecting him, fell a Singing and num-bering them; when looking round me, what should I see but mine Host stript stark-naked, and his Cloaths lying by the High-way-side. The sight struck me every where, and I stood as if I had been dead; but he Piss'd round his Cloaths, and of a sudden was turned to a Wolf: Don't think I jest, I value no Man's Estate at that rate, as to tell a Lye. But as I was saying, after he was turned to a Wolf, he set up a Howl, and fled to the Woods. At first I knew not where I was, till going to take up his Cloaths, I found them also turn'd to Stone. Another Man would have dy'd for fear, but I drew my Sword, and slaying all the Ghosts that came in my way, lighted at last on the place where my Mistress was: I entred the first Door; my eyes were sunk in my Head, the Sweat ran off me by more streams than one, and I was just breathing my last, without thought of recovery; when my Melissa coming to me, began to wonder why I'd be walking so late; and 'if,' said she, 'you had come a little sooner, you might have done us a kindness; for a Wolf came into the Farm, and has made Butchers work enough among the Cattle; but tho' he got off, he has no reason to laugh, for a Servant of ours ran him through the

Neck with a Pitch-fork.' As soon as I had heard her, I could not hold open my Eyes any longer, and ran home by Daylight, like a Vintner whose House had been robb'd: But coming by the place where the Cloaths were turned to Stone, I saw nothing but a Puddle of Blood; and when I got home, found mine Host lying a-bed like an Oxe in his Stall, and a Chirurgeon dressing his Neck. I understood afterwards he was a Fellow that could change his Skin; but from that day forward, could never eat a bit of Bread with him, no if you'd have kill'd me. Let them that don't believe me, examine the truth of it; may your good Angels plague me as I tell ye a Lye."

— *Translated by William Burnaby*

How to Recognize a Werewolf

HOW WOULD WE recognize a werewolf if we saw one? The answer to that might seem simple enough to anyone who has seen a movie like *The Wolf Man* or *Curse of the Were-wolf* or *Legend of the Werewolf*, because here the creature resembles an over-hirsute man with large lupine teeth, growling voice and foam-

ing mouth, and it viciously attacks (but never actually consumes) its victim. But the sort of beast which was portrayed by Lon Chaney, Jr., Oliver Reed and David Rintoul on the cinema screen is merely the result of one of the biggest con-tricks ever perpetuated by the film industry. For, historically, a werewolf in its animal shape resembles a large wolf. Hollywood, perhaps in the belief that it is difficult to make a wolf *act*, stuck yak's hair onto an actor and passed this off as the real thing; and by so doing gave birth to the popular myth of the twentieth-century werewolf. It is pure fancy. If it is your misfortune to bump into a werewolf, and you are not sure whether it is a human being or a real wolf, there is, according to tradition, one infallible test. You should throw steel or iron at the animal under suspicion, whereupon, if it is a genuine werewolf, the skin will split crosswise on the forehead and the man will come out naked through the opening. This "werewolf test" obviously stems from the medieval belief that suspected werewolves have their fur growing on the inside of their skin and that they become werewolves by simply turning themselves inside out.

Countless fully documented trials tell of prisoners who were closely interrogated as to how this inversion was accomplished. As far as I know, none of them gave a convincing answer. At the moment of change, their memories seem to have become temporarily befogged. Now and then a poor devil had his arms and legs cut off, or was partially flayed, in an attempt to detect the ingrowing hair. But I cannot find a scrap of evidence to suggest that the torturers ever found the ingrowing hair they so desperately needed in order to "prove" their case against the convicted werewolves. When one considers that a werewolf in his animal form looks like any other wolf—except that he might be larger and more savage and voracious than ordinary wolves—the problem of how to recognize one is difficult.

In his animals form the head, claws and hairy skin are like those of a real wolf, but he retains his human voice. The surest test of the werewolf's identity, however, lies in his complete absence of a tail. A tendency to transform is believed to wax and wane with the seasons and to be subject to the influence of the moon. His clothes, too, are sure to be found not far from the scene of slaughter.

A strange impediment, which is found in many historical accounts, is that the werewolf falls down quite a lot. This may have something to do with physical exhaustion, because the werewolf also seems to be constantly thirsty. Many of the werewolves in Hungary and the Balkan countries, for instance, were said to be witches who became wolves in order to suck the blood of men who were born during the night of a full moon; by so doing they preserved their health. In their human form they apparently had "pale, sunken faces, hollow eyes, swollen lips, and flabby, weak arms," and after their blood-baths they experienced an acute thirst.

According to some accounts, the werewolf is sometimes frozen with the cold, and on such occasions he is invulnerable to ordinary weapons. The traditional way to wound him is to shoot at him with balls of eider pith or, since we have advanced some-what from the days of the powder-and-ball flintlock, with bullets of inherited silver.

A valuable eye-witness account of a suspected werewolf attack in the Jura Moun-tains in 1598 is given by the infamous judge Henry Boguet in his famous *Discours des Sorciers* (1608). He describes how a fifteen-year-old boy named Benedict climbed a tree one day to pick some fruit when he saw a wolf attacking his younger sister, who was playing at the foot of the tree. He instantly descended the tree to try to protect her with a knife he was carrying, but the wolf quickly turned on him and, with a fierce blow of its paw, tore the knife out of his hand and drove it into his throat. Before he died from the mortal wound, however, Benedict was able to offer a description of the wolf which attacked him. Its forepaws were shaped like human hands, covered on top with thick, bushy hair, while its hind feet were completely covered with fur. A young and demented girl, Perrenette Gandillon, later confessed to the crime and admitted that she was a werewolf, after which she was torn limb from limb by the community. The Gandillons were a particularly loathsome family, and several of them were arrested on charges of sorcery and werewolfery. In prison they behaved as though they were possessed, walking on all fours and howling like wild beasts.

Page 2 A man witnesses a friend attacked by a werewolf, in a woodcut from Johann Geiler von Kaiserberg's *Die Emeis*, 1516.

Page 7 A werewolf ripping after a man's throat from Sabine Baring-Gould's 1865 *The Book of Were-Wolves*.

Page 14 Title page of the 1832 edition of the legend *The Ancient English Romance of William and the Werewolf*, by Frederick Madden. The book was adapted from a fourteenth-century manuscript.

Page 24 The classic werewolf, from an eighteenth-century engraving.

Page 29 King Lycaon, because of his crimes, was transformed into a wolf by Jupiter.

Page 38–39 Seventeenth-century woodcuts for the German fable *The Life and Death of Peter Stump*.

Page 53 The Devil marking an initiate werewolf, from Francesco Maria Guazzo's *Compendium Maleficarum* (1608).

Page 62 Instruments of torture used on accused werewolves in the sixteenth and seventeenth centuries. The suspects were ripped limb by limb to expose the hair supposedly growing on the inside of their flesh.

LORD BYRON's legendary good looks and unerring debauchery earned him a rather wolfish reputation in his day. He perished in 1824 while aiding the Greek fight for independence and is still considered a hero in that country.

A disciple of Gustave Flaubert, **GUY DE MAUPASSANT** (1850–93) published more than two hundred short stories in his lifetime. "The Wolf" was written in 1887.

ANGELA CARTER's surreal adaptations of folk tales are nowhere more present than in her collection *The Bloody Chamber*, from which this story is selected. The novelist, short-story writer, translator and teacher died in 1992.

Interest in **OVID** (43 B.C. – A.D. 18) was revived after the eleventh century, before which his writings were considered "pagan" and read surreptitiously. This selection from his *Metamorphosis* is one of the earliest werewolf stories.

STUBBE PEETER was executed on Halloween 1589 in Bedbur, Germany, for the murder of thirteen children while in the form of a wolf. According to the transcript of his trial reproduced here, the Devil was the culprit.

SAKI, or Hector Hugh Munro (1870–1916), is known primarily for his macabre and ironic short stories. He was born in Burma, educated in England, and died from sniper fire in World War I.

The included **CHARMS AND SPELLS** reportedly turned man into wolf. The litany was repeated at midnight in the moon's full light over a boiling cauldron of opium, hemlock and parsley.

ROBERT BAYFIELD was a seventeenth-century British physician with an interest in both medicine and metaphysics. His cure for wolf-madness tries to combine both, but seems to fall just short.

BRAM STOKER published the wildly popular *Dracula* in 1897. Few know, however, that his publishers forced him to cut the first chapter from the book, feeling it was too long. That chapter—"Dracula's Guest"—is reprinted here.

PETRONIUS is traditionally identified with Gaius Petronius Arbiter, a one-time favorite of Emperor Nero. Nero's change of mind led to Petronius' forced suicide in A.D. 65.

IAN WOODWARD is the author of the 1979 tome *The Were-wolf Delusion*, from which this excerpt is taken.

ACKNOWLEDGMENTS

"The Werewolf" from *The Bloody Chamber and Other Adult Tales* by Angela Carter, ©1979 by Angela Carter. Reprinted by permission of HarperCollins Publishers, Inc.